A friendship so sublime.

written and illustrated by
Wendi Tooth

A friendship so sublime.

ISBN: 978-7356284-2-4

Sitting in the dark till the early morn,
Coffee sits waiting for the wake up horn.

Perched there overnight, listening to me sleep,
Thinking I'm awake with every "PEEP".

Walking to the kitchen, I feel a little perk,
I can hear Coffee's busy and the magic at work.

As I get closer, the sound of the drip,
Waiting to gift me the first filtered sip.

"Good morning Coffee!" I say with a smile,
I can tell by the grin, they've been waiting awhile.

I pick Coffee up and give a great big hug,
They hug me back with that warm shiny mug.

When I set Coffee down, a whimper's all I hear,
But, we've just begun, my sweet roasted dear.

We talk about the night and tell of our dreams,
Time flies by, like hours it always seems.

Coffee can see something is on my mind,
But I don't leave them, my hot tempered grind.

Looking out the window, or perched on my knee,
Coffee will always be riding with me.

We always make the best of our time,
Laughing together, a friendship so sublime.
Shhh...!

But sometimes I have to let Coffee go,
Like in the shower, on the toilet, or out for a mow.

Coffee can get mad and get kind of bitter,
"Almost done, my silly mini jitter!"

They're right, life's better with them around,
They keep me balanced, they're the perfect ground.

Like when I need to study, read, and write,
They keep me company all through the night.

Or the early mornings I'm up with the sun,
Especially before my 5k run.

So smart and always knowing what to do,
A good lunch mate, my groovy brewed dude.

Life would be so dull without this teeny bean,
Every minute together keeps my mind so keen.

A pal by my side, never gone for good,
A cup filler for all, if only they could.

Always to be found, never out of reach,
Corner store, mountain tops, down to the beach.

A social bug, a joyous meeting surprise,
A birthday party must, and a gift card prize.

Best to be careful and not let them spill,
They'll make a huge mess, that strong Coffee will.

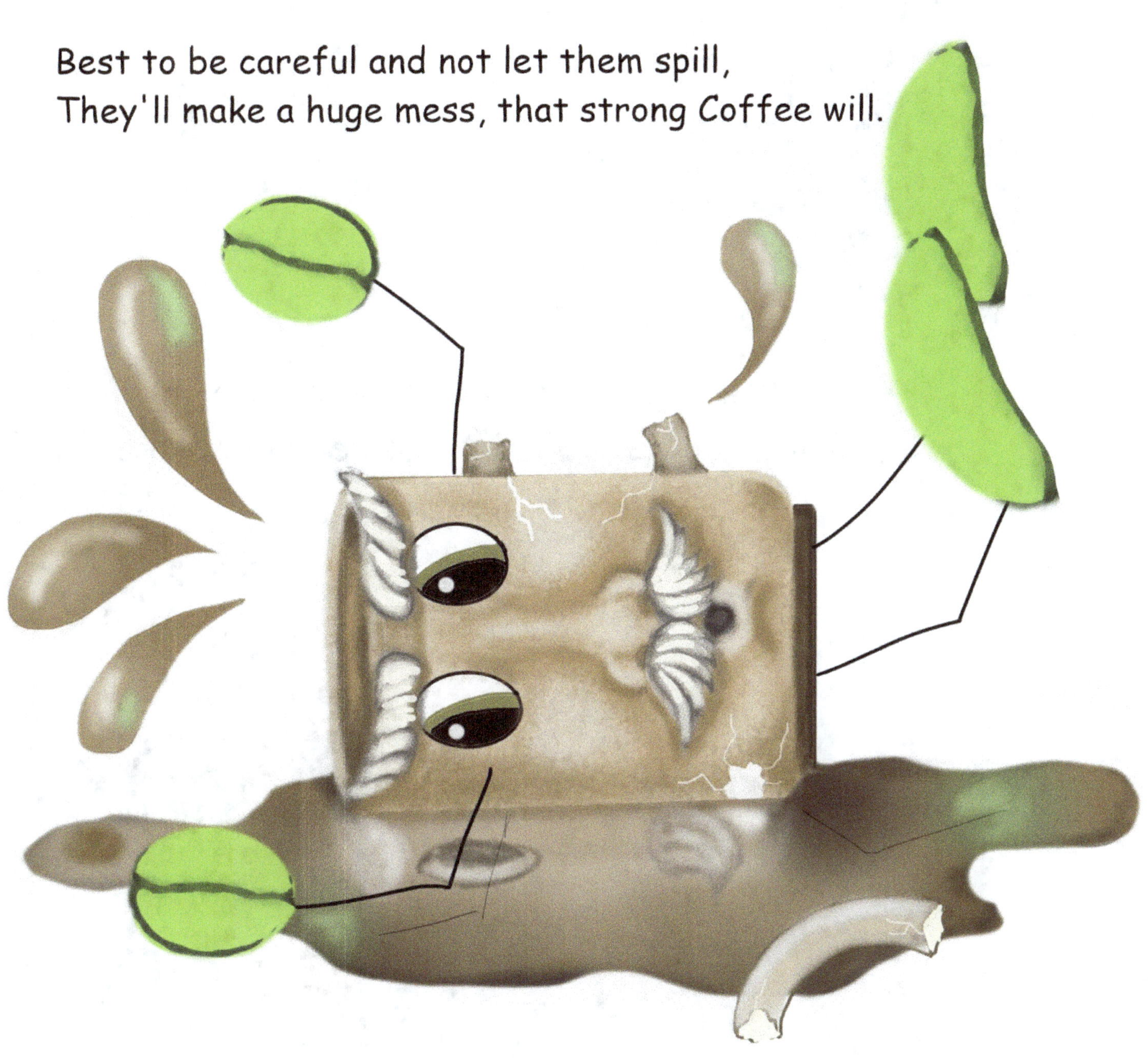

Coffee can get cold and need a warm wrap,
They can get too hot and really act like crap!

They'll refuse to admit, the java friend,
They get worn and tired too, at the days end.

But not for long, they'll gladly perk right up,
Willing and ready, that wired caffeine cup!

So on bad days or feeling a bit slow,
A Coffee is best, your own cup of joe.

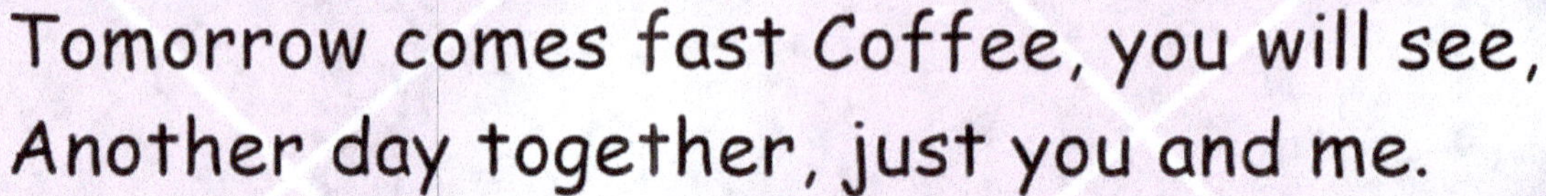
Tomorrow comes fast Coffee, you will see,
Another day together, just you and me.

www.ingramcontent.com/pod-product-compliance
Lightning Source LLC
Chambersburg PA
CBHW080811020826
48982CB00017B/868

* 9 7 8 1 7 3 5 6 2 8 4 2 4 *